Sept. 26, 2014

DEAREST CARA
IN
WONDERFULAND

Dear John,

Greetings from Wonderfuland!

Patty ☺

By Patty Harmsen
Illustrated by Cara Harmsen

© Patty Harmsen

ISBN: 978-81-7896-110-1

First Edition : December 2013

Bahá'í Publishing Trust
F-3/6, Okhla Industrial Area, Phase-I
New Delhi-110020, India

Printed at: JK Offset Graphic Pvt. Ltd.

*This book is dedicated to my father Gene Smith
who gave his children the gift of imagination.
A very special thank you to
Cara, Craig, Hans, Rick and Wandra
for all their love, support and encouragement.*

Table of Contents

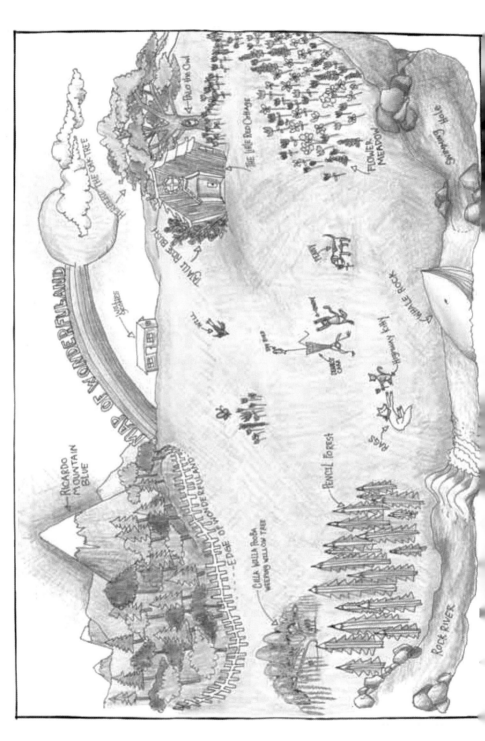

Chapter 1

Wonderfuland

Wonderfuland is a place of much beauty, peacefulness and love. Within its meadows, mountains, and trees live many furry woodland creatures and special animal friends. The meadow is dotted with beautiful wild flowers of all different sizes, colors and shapes. Some are tall, some are small. Their colors vary from yellow to pink, to orange, red and purple. The flowers make Wonderfuland smell so wonderful! The Rock River wraps around the edge of Wonderfuland creating many little waterfalls and deep swimming holes. On the bank of the river is an enormous rounded stone. It is so big that its humongous shape looks like a whale. This stone is known as Whale Rock throughout all of Wonderfuland.

In the south of Wonderfuland there is a forest named Pencil Forest. It is named this because of the tall and thin pine trees that reach far up into the sky and resemble pencils from a distance. Among the many trees in Pencil Forest, there is one very special tree that lives on its edge. This tree is named Cilla Willa Pooba. She is a weeping willow tree. She is tall and strong and has many branches reaching out alongside of her trunk with bright green leaves that are long and slender. She is famous for giving wonderful loving hugs with her long-branch arms.

Past Pencil Forest and over the Rock River to the north is a mountain known as Ricardo Mountain Blue. Tall, majestic, and pointed at the very top, Ricardo Mountain Blue casts a deep blue color in the sky when the sun goes down. This creates a peaceful feeling and makes everyone happy in Wonderfuland.

A little red cottage sits on a hill that overlooks the meadow and the Rock River. Everyone knows the little red cottage from far away by the huge chimney made of large round rocks taken from the Rock River. The family that lives in this little red cottage has an eight year-old daughter named Dearest Cara. She is a very happy child and lives with her Momsy and Poppy and her many pets and animal friends. Some of these animals live with the family. The others live in the forests and meadows of Wonderfuland.

When guests visit Dearest Cara's family, they are greeted by a large beautiful rose bush growing along the side of the cottage. Momsy loves this rose bush very much and has given it a special name: Tajalli Rose. This rose bush has bright crimson red blossoms that continually bloom throughout the summer. These blossoms make the inside and outside of the cottage smell like rose perfume...mmmmmmm, heavenly!

On the back side of the cottage is a big old oak tree with large leaves and gigantic acorns. The family named it 'Herbert the Oak', because of its strong large trunk and sturdy thick branches. It has a deep wide hole in the upper part of the trunk where animals can make a nice cozy home.

Chapter 2

Dearest Cara

Dearest Cara has many beautiful qualities, virtues, and special talents! She also has a very unique gift that lets her talk to animals. She understands the language and feelings of all the animals that live in Wonderfuland and has a very close bond with each and every one of them. Before Dearest Cara was born, the animals of Wonderfuland had never met a human that loved them so much and understood them so deeply.

Dearest Cara has great big blue eyes, the color of the ocean, and long golden-blond pigtails high up on each side of her head.

Momsy often puts wild flowers from the meadow or crimson red roses from Tajalli Rose bush in Dearest Cara's hair.

Dearest Cara has so much energy! She loves to sing, dance, run and leap through the flowers of the meadow in Wonderfuland with all her animal friends trailing behind her. On sunny days Dearest Cara jumps from stone to stone in the Rock River or picks beautiful flowers to make a bouquet for Momsy. One of Dearest Cara's favorite activities is to climb up Cilla Willa Pooba, the weeping willow tree, and let Cilla Willa Pooba wrap her long-branch arms around her so she can give Dearest Cara a great big loving warm hug!

You may also find Dearest Cara at her most favorite place in Wonderfuland, Whale Rock. Dearest Cara likes to go to this spot to sit and have quiet time on bright sunny days. On top of Whale Rock Dearest Cara prays for guidance and assistance and to thank God for her many blessings. For Dearest Cara, Whale Rock is so peaceful that sometimes she just sits quietly, listening to the sound of the water as it flows over the stones and little waterfalls of the Rock River.

Dearest Cara has some very special animal friends. They are always right by her side or only a yodel call away. These animal friends have many interesting stories. Each story tells about how they came to live at Wonderfuland and what virtues they and Dearest Cara learn in their adventures together.

Chapter 3

Palo and the Virtue of Generosity

Every night before Dearest Cara goes to sleep, she looks out of her bedroom window and talks to an owl named Palo. At sunset Palo perches on a branch of Herbert the Oak outside her window and Dearest Cara tells Palo all about her day, the fun things that happened, the good choices she made, as well as some of the choices that may have caused problems. Most importantly, Palo always asks Dearest Cara about a virtue she has learned and practiced that day. Palo is very wise and then shares a Bahá'í teaching about that virtue. How Dearest Cara met Palo is a very interesting tale. This is the story of how their friendship began.

One night, before Momsy and Poppy came into Dearest Cara's bedroom to say prayers before bedtime, Dearest Cara was looking out of her window. She was thinking about her day as she gazed upward at all the sparkling stars in the dark night sky. She began to talk out loud to herself about her day. As she was looking at the stars and talking, a voice out of nowhere suddenly talked back to her.

9

The voice said, "You've had an interesting day young lady."

Dearest Cara looked about and in a puzzled voice exclaimed, "Who said that!?!"

"Why I did young Miss. Please allow me to introduce myself. My name is Palo and I'm an owl. Please forgive me if I frightened you."

Dearest Cara turned to her side and saw an owl with feathers of dark brown and golden stripes and big black eyes. He was perched on a nearby branch of Herbert the Oak and was observing Dearest Cara with much curiosity.

Dearest Cara with a very excited voice replied, "You did not scare me Palo. I'm very happy to meet you. My name is Dearest Cara."

Palo made a small bow and said, "I hope you do not mind that I'm sitting on this branch. You see, I just stopped to rest because I'm in search of a new home."

"What happened to your home?" Dearest Cara asked with much concern.

Palo in a sad and quiet voice said, "I come from up north, many miles away from Wonderfuland. One day lumberjacks came into the forest and cut down all the trees to make way for a new highway. My home was destroyed."

Dearest Cara felt her heart ache with sadness when Palo said that he was homeless.

Dearest Cara looked into Palo's big brown owl eyes and said, "Palo, please stay and make Wonderfuland your new home. You can live in Herbert the Oak. There's an opening that leads to a deep hole inside the tree. It would make a perfect home for an owl. Herbert is a strong old tree and no one will ever cut him down."

Dearest Cara continued excitedly, "We can talk every night before I go to bed and I can tell you all about my day and adventures in Wonderfuland!"

Palo lifted one eyebrow and thought about Dearest Cara's offer. After a short time Palo scratched his head with his wing and said, "Well,

I think I'd like this very much Dearest Cara. Thank you! I'll make Herbert the Oak tree my new home. Your offer is very *generous*. In one of my Bahá'í books, Bahá'u'lláh speaks about the virtue of *generosity*. Do you know what Bahá'u'lláh says about *generosity*?"

"No." replied Dearest Cara in a very curious tone.

"Bahá'u'lláh says, *to give and to be generous are attributes of Mine; well is it with him that adorneth himself with My virtues.*"

Dearest Cara then asked, "Palo, what's a *virtue*?"

Palo answered, "*Virtues* are spiritual qualities that we try to strengthen within ourselves during our life. Bahá'u'lláh has told us to always work on developing virtues within ourselves, like you just did by practicing the virtue of *generosity*. You're very *generous* to offer me a place to live here at Wonderfuland! If you think it would be helpful, every evening before you go to bed we can discuss a *virtue* you've practiced and learned about that day."

Dearest Cara said with much excitement, "I'd like that very much Palo!"

Then Dearest Cara leaned over and asked in a very concerned voice, "What might you need to make your new home comfy Palo?"

Palo replied with a big smile, "Well Dearest Cara, you're being very *generous* again. I was not able to bring very much with me except a backpack filled with my Bahá'í books. These include my prayer book and spiritual writings from Bahá'u'lláh and `Abdu'l-Bahá. Since I am an owl, I like to stay up and read my books during the night. I suppose—if it's not too much trouble—a curtain to keep the sunlight out during the day when I sleep would be very useful. I'd appreciate this very much Dearest Cara."

"No trouble at all Palo, that's easy!" she answered with much excitement. "Just a minute and I'll be right back!" Dearest Cara ran out of the bedroom to find an old curtain Momsy had tucked away in the attic.

That evening Palo settled into his new home in Herbert the Oak right next to Dearest Cara's bedroom window. Palo was so happy and grateful to have found a new home in Wonderfuland and to have made a very special new friend in Dearest Cara!

Dearest Cara was so happy to have found a new friend who she could talk with every night before she went to sleep. So happy!

Chapter 4

Penny and the Virtue of Patience

Dearest Cara's family adopted Penny as a puppy from a gentle elderly couple. Two important things about Penny are that she has a 'super-duper sniffer' nose and she is crazy about food. Do you know what Penny said to Dearest Cara the day she came to live at Wonderfuland? She said, "This place smells great! ...like candy-corn and pumpkin pie!"

While Penny can be adorable, she can also be a little cranky when she cannot have her own way.

When she is cranky it usually has something to do with food. When she gets grumpy, she lets out a low rumbling growl and grumbles and mumbles under her breath. But even when Penny is being a grump, Dearest Cara tries to be *patient* with her since she is still a puppy and always learning.

Sometimes Penny's appetite and her 'super-duper sniffer' get the best of her. For

instance, shortly after Penny arrived, Poppy was baking Dearest Cara's most favorite pie...pecan pie. This delicious dessert also happened to be Penny's favorite pie as well.

Dearest Cara, her best friend Michelle, and a few of the other animal friends— Penny, a dog named Rags, two cats named Sparky and Highway Kitty and two birds named Sky and Will—were all out and about playing and laughing in Pencil Forest. Poppy had been cooking all day and had placed a freshly baked pecan pie on the kitchen windowsill to cool. Being a breezy autumn day, the smell of the freshly baked pie wafted over the meadow and among the pine trees of Pencil Forest.

When Penny's 'super-duper sniffer' caught a whiff of the freshly baked pecan pie, she froze and her eyes began spinning around in circles! Penny's nose started to follow the smell of the pecan goodness and she began to stray from the group. Dearest Cara looked over at Penny and noticed that she had strayed and was acting very strange.

She blurted out in a high pitched tone, "Penny! You've got googley-eyes! What's going on, do you smell something with your 'super-duper sniffer'?"

Penny's tongue was hanging out and she was panting very loudly. In between her gasps for air she sputtered, "Dearest Cara... pecan pie...close by...*gabba, gabba, gabba!*"

Dearest Cara began thinking about the sweet brown sugary taste of Poppy's homemade pecan pies with their big crunchy pecans and sweet gooey filling. Her eyes opened wide and beamed with great excitement, "Pecan pie? Why if that isn't my most favorite pie in the whole wide world! Michelle, do you smell that pecan pie?!!"

"I sure do!" declared Michelle.

Dearest Cara shouted, "Lead the way Penny and help us find that pecan pie!!"

Well, before you knew it, Penny, Dearest Cara and Michelle were running as fast as they could, over the meadow, up the hill and toward the little red cottage where the delicious pecan pie was cooling on the windowsill.

The other animals, Rags, Sparky, Highway Kitty, Sky and Will ran behind them, each yelling out as loud as they could, "Stop! Stop! Come back! Don't eat the pie; you've got to ask Momsy's and Poppy's permission!"

Will, the bright red cardinal, flew up quickly beside Dearest Cara head. He was flapping his wings so hard and fast it created a strong wind that blew Dearest Cara's bangs straight up on her head! Will cried out, "Dearest Cara, please wait! You must be *patient* and wait until Momsy serves the pecan pie after dinner so everyone can have a piece!"

But it was no use. Penny, Dearest Cara and Michelle kept running until they reached the windowsill where the yummy pecan pie was cooling. Penny leaped through the air, grabbed the pecan pie and broke it into two halves. She kept one half for herself and threw the other half to Dearest Cara and Michelle. Penny started gobbling down the pie and in between the slurps and chews you could hear her singing, "*Yummy, yummy, yummy I got pecan pie in my tummy*! Oh, how I love Pecan Pie! Delicious! Oh happy day!"

Dearest Cara and Michelle were also enjoying their pieces of the pie as well. Through mouthfuls of gooey pecan filling and crumbling buttery pie crust, Dearest Cara would blurt out with much excitement, "This pie is scrump-dilly-icious!"

Now there is an old dog named Sammy that lives in the cottage with Dearest Cara and her family. Sammy came to Wonderfuland many years before Dearest Cara was born. Sammy has lived for many years in Wonderfuland and thinks of himself as a sheriff whose duty it is to keep the peace between the animal friends. But, since he is so old he mostly spends his days sleeping in the sunroom or stretched out on the warm grass.

All the noise and commotion brought Sammy out of a deep sleep. He jumped up from the rug in the sunroom and came outside of the little red cottage to see what all the hubbub was about.

As he came upon Dearest Cara, Michelle and Penny, stuffing their faces with pie, he let out a loud slow bark while looking straight at the three pie-burglars.

In a stern voice and holding up his paw, Sammy shouted, "STOP in the name of the *PAW*!"

Penny pretended not to hear Sammy and kept devouring the pie. She continued to eat with such speed that you might have thought she was trying to come in first place in a pie-eating contest!

Dearest Cara and Michelle froze in place at the sound of Sammy's command. With mouths full of pie and brown sugary crumbs all over their faces, they both suddenly realized what they had done.

Dearest Cara quickly turned around and looked at Penny and placed her hand on the puppy's shoulder. Dearest Cara tried to shake her and free her from the pie-eating trance. Dearest Cara shouted, "Penny, stop eating the pie!! We've done something very wrong. Snap out of it Penny!"

But it was too late. In one final gulp, Penny devoured the rest of the pecan pie and licked the last remaining crumbs of the pecan filling out of the pie pan. She looked up at everyone and let out a small burp.

Right about this time, Momsy came outside to see why Sammy was barking. With pecan pie filling all over their faces, hands, and paws, it was plain as day. Penny, Dearest Cara, and Michelle had eaten the pecan pie on the windowsill!

Momsy asked in a shocked voice, "What in the world is going on here Dearest Cara?! What have you, Michelle and that crazy beagle done?! Poppy had made that pecan pie for everyone to eat after dinner!"

Momsy, very upset continued, "Now there is no pecan pie for anyone! If you had been *patient*, everyone would have had a slice of pie after dinner. But now, *no one* will have any pie. I'm very disappointed with all three of you!"

Momsy left Dearest Cara, Michelle and Penny to think about what they had done. All three of them had sad and ashamed looks on their faces.

With no dessert after dinner that evening, Dearest Cara, Michelle and Penny went up to Dearest Cara's bedroom. As they looked out of the window, they began to watch the sunset. Ricardo Mountain Blue cast a peaceful blue hue over Wonderfuland. Palo was perched on a nearby branch. He noticed Dearest Cara's face and how very sad she looked. Tears began to fill the corners of Dearest Cara's eyes. Dearest Cara and Michelle told Palo all about the pecan pie caper and how Momsy was very disappointed with the three of them.

Palo listened to the whole story and then replied, "Dearest Cara and Michelle, we must all try to be *patient*...We can't have everything we want, right when we want it. When we practice the virtue of *patience*, our will becomes stronger and this pleases God."

"I don't understand." replied Dearest Cara with a sad tone.

With a smile and a soft voice Palo replied, "*Patience* is a virtue of God. He has given the spiritual quality of *patience* to us as a gift. The virtue of *patience* helps us to wait for something. For example, think about when you want something so much that you actually believe you can't live without it. *Patience* helps us to wait and accept that we can't have everything we want exactly when we want it. In doing this we learn to accept God's Will and become detached from earthly things. This strengthens our own will and makes our spirits strong. Living in this way is the spirit of being a Bahá'í."

24

Dearest Cara thought about Palo's words. "So when I control the feeling of wanting something right away, this is being *patient*?"

"Yes," said Palo.

At that moment Dearest Cara and Michelle agreed to work on strengthening the virtue of *patience* in their daily lives.

Palo continued, "Remember what `Abdu'l-Bahá said, *little by little; day by day*. No one is perfect. We have to try to be a little better each day."

Dearest Cara and Michelle thought more about the virtue of *patience*. They went downstairs to Momsy and Poppy who were sitting in front of the fireplace and apologized for eating the pecan pie without asking first.

After Dearest Cara and Michelle apologized, Penny walked into the room and rolled on her back and whimpered like a big baby. This was her way of showing that she was also very sorry for what she had done. Momsy and Poppy were very pleased to see that everyone involved in the shenanigans had realized their wrong-doings and learned from their mistakes.

In the end, Penny, Dearest Cara and Michelle received their just desserts: they all had stomach aches when they went to bed that night from eating too much pecan pie. But even with their stomach aches, they felt grateful to have such a warm, loving and forgiving family. And with this feeling of gratitude they all drifted peacefully into sleep.

Chapter 5

Sparky and the Virtue of Kindness

One spring morning, Dearest Cara and Poppy stopped by the animal shelter in the nearby city of Springfield. They had come to the shelter to drop off some containers of homemade peanut butter dog biscuits that Poppy had helped Dearest Cara bake. They had made the dog biscuits the day before as a service project that was part of Dearest Cara's Bahá'í children's class.

The animal shelter was very happy for the donation of biscuits. After Dearest Cara and Poppy finished bringing in the last container and were getting ready to leave, Dearest Cara thought she heard a faint meow coming from the back room of the shelter. Poking her head around the door to see where the mewing was coming from, she saw one of the volunteers from the shelter feeding a small kitten with a tiny bottle of milk. The little kitten could barely keep his eyes open. Its fur was all black except for a small white triangle located on his stomach that made the kitten look like it was wearing a diaper!

The volunteer noticed Dearest Cara standing in the doorway looking intently at the kitten and invited her in. The volunteer smiled at her and explained, "This little guy is all that is left of a litter of kittens that was brought in the other day. All his brothers and sisters have been adopted."

Dearest Cara walked over to the kitten and scooped it into her arms and it immediately began to purr. It was love at first purr and Dearest Cara knew this kitten needed a home. Cradling the little furball in her arms like a baby, Dearest Cara walked out of the back room and asked Poppy if this little kitty could come home with them.

Poppy saw how happy the little kitten was, lying on his back in Dearest Cara's arms. Poppy laughed and said, "It looks like that little kitten has already adopted *you*, Dearest Cara! Yes, he can come back with us to Wonderfuland."

Dearest Cara held up the little kitten and laughed as she looked into its face, "I'm going to call you Sparky! You'll be my little *sparkazoid!*" Sparky smiled and closed his eyes and purred very loudly to show how happy he was.

There is something Dearest Cara discovered about Sparky as he got older. He is a very interesting cat, to say the least, and only Dearest Cara truly understands him. When guests come to visit Wonderfuland, Sparky will run up to them and rub against their legs. But just as the guest bends down to pet Sparky, he looks up at them with a glaring eye and lets out a great big growl and hiss. This in turn makes the guest jump backwards while letting out a big, loud yelp!

Dearest Cara says Sparky does this because he likes to be in charge of who pets him. Momsy understands and respects how Sparky feels. However, she would like him not to do this every time a visitor comes to the cottage.

One summer day, Dearest Cara invited one of her best friends, Jen, to a sleepover at Wonderfuland. That night, Jen slept in Sparky's favorite place on Dearest Cara's bed. This made Sparky very upset. The next morning when Jen awoke, she felt breaths of hot air on her face. She opened one eye very slowly to see where the hot air was coming from. Sparky's glaring eyes were one inch from her face. Sparky was so angry, that his whiskers were vibrating!

Jen, fearing for her life, quickly jumped out of bed and shrieked, "Dearest Cara wake up! Sparky's gone *loco*!"

As Jen's feet hit the floor, Sparky pushed off the bed, wrapped himself around Jen's ankle and began swatting at her other foot with his paw.

Sparky hung on with all his might and would not let go. Jen shouted for help. In a shrill voice, she cried, "Dearest Cara!!! Sparky's got my leg and won't let go!"

Jen started running around the room shaking her leg like she was doing a disco dance, hoping Sparky would fall off. But Sparky hung on with all his might, as if his very life depended on it!

Dearest Cara woke up from the commotion and could not believe her eyes. She yelled, "Sparky, let go!!! *Let go of Jen's leg right now!!!*"

Sparky would not listen and hung onto Jen's leg. Momsy, hearing all the yelling, ran into the room to see what all the hullabaloo was about. She saw what Sparky was doing and in a very stern voice ordered, "Sparky stop this immediately! Let go of Jen's leg!"

Sparky finally relented and let go. Dearest Cara told Sparky to take a 'time out' in the other room and think about what he had done. Sparky slowly walked out of Dearest Cara's room and let out a snort under his breath.

That evening Dearest Cara and Sparky went to her bedroom window to think about the events of their day. Dearest Cara told Palo about what happened with Sparky and Jen.

Dearest Cara reflected on the morning and said, "I understand why Sparky was upset about Jen sleeping in his favorite spot. I didn't ask Sparky if he would share his spot with Jen before she came over, but I also know that it's important to be polite and *kind* when guests come to our home. I'm worried that Sparky might do this again the next time Jen sleeps over."

Palo pondered Dearest Cara's words and responded, "Dearest Cara, the next time Jen sleeps over, why not have Sparky sleep on the other side of the bed next to you?"

Palo then turned to Sparky and said, "Remember Sparky, we can't always have our own way. It's important to practice the virtue of *kindness* and have good manners when guests come to our house."

"'Abdu'l-Bahá says, *be kind to all people and love them with a pure spirit.*"

Sparky nodded his head and said, "Okay. I'll try to be *kind* and polite with guests and share my spot on the bed the next time Jen sleeps over."

Palo added, "That also means not hissing at them when they pet you."

Sparky seemed genuinely shocked. "What!?!?! Well, okay," he replied with disappointment.

Dearest Cara hugged Sparky and said, "Next time, I'll let you know the day before when Jen will be sleeping over. That way, we can have time to fix up a cozy spot for you on the other side of the bed. Momsy always says when we make mistakes we have to learn from them and try to do better the next time."

Sparky nodded his furry head and took his front paws and wrapped them around Dearest Cara's shoulder giving her a great big hug! That night Sparky snuggled up next to Dearest Cara and purred until he drifted off to sleep.

Chapter 6

Highway Kitty and the Virtue of Compassion

One evening, Dearest Cara was driving home with Momsy from a Feast at one of the Bahá'í Friend's home in a nearby town. As they were getting close to Wonderfuland, Dearest Cara spotted a very tiny kitten limping and dragging her front paw on the side of the road. When Dearest Cara saw the little kitten, she shouted, "Momsy, quick! Please stop the car! There's a kitten on the side of the road and it looks like it's badly hurt!"

Momsy, who also loves animals very much, carefully and quickly pulled the car over and stopped on the side of the road. Dearest Cara jumped out of the car and scooped up the little kitten in her arms. She took off her sweater and wrapped the kitten up like a new born baby. They named her Highway Kitty and brought her to a veterinarian who put a cast on Highway Kitty's front paw. After a few weeks they returned to the vet to take the cast off. Although the bone had healed, Highway Kitty still walked with a limp. To this day she still drags her left front paw when she walks.

Since Highway Kitty cannot run very fast like the other animals friends, Dearest Cara frequently carries Highway Kitty in her arms or on her shoulder while she runs in the meadow. Dearest Cara always takes care to make sure Highway Kitty does not get left behind.

Sometimes Highway Kitty feels sad about not being able keep up with the other animal friends when they run through the meadow. When this happens, Dearest Cara comforts Highway Kitty and tells her, "Even though you walk with a limp and can't run very fast, it doesn't matter, my sweet little kitty! You're very special just the way you are! Even when running is difficult, you stick with it and you try with all your might!"

Well, when Highway Kitty first came to Wonderfuland, can you guess who was jealous? If you guessed Sparky, you were right! Sparky was a bit jealous.....well maybe more than just a bit. He was *extremely* jealous!

Dearest Cara tried very hard to help Sparky to get to know and love Highway Kitty who was so tiny, scared and injured when she first arrived at Wonderfuland. On Highway Kitty's first evening in Wonderfuland, Dearest Cara and Sparky sat together looking out of Dearest Cara's bedroom window. Palo was perched on a nearby branch of Herbert the Oak.

Dearest Cara said to Palo, "Sparky is having a hard time with Highway Kitty living in Wonderfuland. I think he's feeling jealous about Highway Kitty."

Sparky curled up the side of his mouth, which caused his whiskers to stand straight up in the air and said in a very annoyed voice, "Why does that kitten get all the attention around here? She even moved onto my spot on Dearest Cara's bed!"

Palo looked at Sparky and raised an eyebrow. "Sparky, I believe you think the whole bed is your *spot*."

Sparky looked back at Palo and said with an angry snort, "That's right! The whole bed *is my spot.*"

Palo tilted his head and looked Sparky square in the eyes. "Highway Kitty is very sick and little. We must have *compassion* for her and do everything we can to help her recover. Sparky, remember what `Abdu'l-Bahá said to the early believers: *be a cause of healing for every sick one, a comforter for every sorrowful one...*"

Later that night Sparky thought about the words of 'Abdu'l-Bahá as he drifted into sleep. He was still feeling annoyed that Highway Kitty was sleeping on *his* and Dearest Cara's bed.

The next morning Sparky got up and went downstairs to have breakfast. Shortly after, Dearest Cara got out of bed and decided to go to Whale Rock to say healing prayers for Highway Kitty's recovery. Before she left, she tucked Highway Kitty into a fluffy pink blanket at the foot of her bed.

After his breakfast of kitty cereal with fresh cream that Momsy had prepared for him, Sparky went back upstairs to Dearest Cara's room to take his morning snooze on Dearest Cara's bed. But, when he jumped up onto the bed he found, to his surprise that Highway Kitty was already at the foot of the bed. She was sleeping in his favorite snoozing spot and laying on a fluffy pink blanket...his fluffy pink blanket!

Sparky was beside himself with anger. He let out a giant snort and growled at Highway Kitty. "What do you think you're doing? Move it, kid! *Scram!* This is MY spot."

At that moment, Highway Kitty looked up at Sparky and started crying. She was very weak and felt terrible. As Sparky sat on the bed staring at Highway Kitty, he began to feel badly that he made Highway Kitty cry.

He remembered 'Abdu'l-Bahá's words from the night before.

...Be a cause of healing for every sick one, a comforter for every sorrowful one...

Sparky started to feel a funny feeling inside. His heart began to swell with *compassion* and love for Highway Kitty. In a soft caring voice, Sparky said "Highway Kitty, you sure do look sick and scared."

41

Sparky crept a little closer. He took his paw and tucked the pink blanket around Highway Kitty and cuddled up next to her. He then placed his paw around her shoulder to give her some comfort and make her feel loved. They snuggled together and drifted off to sleep.

About an hour or so later, Dearest Cara came into her bedroom and was very surprised by what she saw! The two kitties were cuddled up together and fast asleep. This made her very happy!

That evening Dearest Cara shared the events of her day with Palo. She told Palo how happy she was to see Sparky treating Highway Kitty with so much love.

Palo was also pleased to hear this news. He said to Dearest Cara, "Sparky is practicing the virtue of *compassion*. He was able to bring Highway Kitty into his heart and feel her pain and sadness."

Dearest Cara wondered and asked, "How do you bring someone into your heart?"

Palo explained, "Bahá'u'lláh tells us that His home is in our hearts. When we imagine bringing someone into our heart with love and *compassion*, we begin to feel the love and *compassion* God feels for every living thing on earth. He helps us to feel *compassion* for others when they're suffering. This makes it easier to be a friend and helper to each other and to be of service to humanity."

Dearest Cara smiled and replied, "Highway Kitty has helped Sparky and I understand the virtue of *compassion* today. I'm very grateful for this."

Dearest Cara looked over at Sparky and Highway Kitty snuggled together on her bed. She could tell that Highway Kitty did not feel scared and did not feel any more pain... only love, sweet love. To this day Sparky and Highway Kitty have a very special bond and enjoy taking long naps together on Dearest Cara's bed.

Chapter 7

Sky Bird and the Virtue of Caring

Dearest Cara was playing tag with a few of the animal friends in the meadow near Pencil Forest. Highway Kitty was on Dearest Cara's shoulder and Penny, Sparky and Rags the dog, were trailing behind, jumping, leaping and laughing in the warm afternoon summer sun.

Suddenly, Penny stopped running and shouted out in a very serious, commanding voice, "Hold everything....everyone stop running! I smell something strange... a birdy! I smell a birdy in the meadow, and something does not smell right!"

Rags looked over at Penny, blurted out a big laugh and in a teasing voice said, "Whatever do you mean Penny! A birdy that does not smell right? What's a birdy supposed to smell like?"

The other animal friends started to giggle too, and Penny shouted again, "Stop laughing! I mean something is wrong with the birdy! I think it's in trouble!"

Dearest Cara looked worried and said, "Penny, can you lead us to the birdy who needs help?"

"I sure will," exclaimed Penny and she put her nose into super-duper turbo-sniffing mode!

Dearest Cara and the animal friends followed Penny as she led them through the meadow and into Pencil Forest. After they ran for a few minutes they found a very tiny baby bird near the gate of Wonderfuland. The little bird was weakly chirping and was half buried under a pile of leaves and twigs.

Rags burst out in a worried voice, "Good gravy, Dearest Cara! Look! A baby bird! It must have fallen out of its nest!"

Dearest Cara and the animal friends circled around a tiny, light blue and white parakeet. The little bird lay shivering and looked very weak and sick. As you might imagine, all the animal friends were very worried and started to offer suggestions on what they should do to help the little bird.

Dearest Cara gently picked up the tiny bird and cradled it her hands and said, "I must take this baby bird to Momsy. She'll know how to heal her."

Rags took off his red bandanna and folded it into a small blanket. He then laid it over the shivering baby bird in Dearest Cara's hands.

With Penny leading the way, Dearest Cara ran and held the baby bird gently but firmly in her hands with Rags and Sparky running beside her. Rags carried Highway Kitty on his back. They ran as fast as they could out of Pencil Forest, through the meadow and up the hill to the little red cottage to find Momsy.

Dearest Cara burst in through the backdoor of the cottage and tried to catch her breath as all the animal friends fell in behind her. She brought the tiny bird into the living room where Momsy was sitting and knitting a scarf.

In a trembling voice Dearest Cara said to her mother, "Momsy! Momsy!... Look what we found... in Pencil Forest...a poor little baby bird... I think she's very sick. *Can you help this baby bird get better Momsy?* Can you *please* help her?"

Momsy took the tiny, sick bird from Dearest Cara's hands and said, "Oh dear, I'll do my best to help this little bird get well, my Dearest Cara!"

"Dearest Cara replied, "Momsy, her feathers are the color of the sky; I think we should name her *Sky!*"

Momsy looked over at Dearest Cara with a loving gaze and replied, "I like that name very much!" Momsy then went into the kitchen and made a special bird food that Dearest Cara fed to Sky with an eye dropper in the days that followed. Momsy also set up a little heat lamp near Sky's bed to keep her warm. During this time the animal friends all took turns keeping watch over Sky to make sure she would not take a turn for the worst.

Dearest Cara went to Whale Rock every day and said healing prayers for Sky. As the days turned into weeks, Sky became stronger and stronger and soon she was able to fly from her cage to a nearby bookcase, and then from room to room. After a few more weeks had passed, Sky had grown strong and learned to fly laps around the little red cottage. This she enjoyed very much to Dearest Cara's delight.

After two months it seemed as if Sky had completely recovered and was stronger than ever. The animal friends gathered in the meadow to watch Sky perform an 'air dance' that was a flying acrobatic dance of summersaults and twirls.

After her performance all the animals cried out a big *hip-hip-hooray!* and all agreed that Sky was a very talented little bird. Dearest Cara held out her finger and Sky landed on it and took a bow.

Chirping a sweet song to Dearest Cara and the animal friends, Sky sang her appreciation for being healed and having Dearest Cara and all the animal friends in her life.

That night Dearest Cara and Palo talked about Sky's miraculous recovery. Palo shared with Dearest Cara how she, Momsy, Penny, Rags, Sparky and Highway Kitty all practiced the virtue of *caring*.

Palo told her that their actions reminded him of what 'Abdu'l-Bahá once said:

It is they who help the poor and needy and give to them their daily bread. They love and care for the sick....

Dearest Cara asked, "Who's "*they*" that 'Abdu'l-Bahá is talking about?

"I believe He's talking about all of us... how we should try to live every day, caring for one another just like 'Abdu'l-Bahá did during his life," answered Palo.

Dearest Cara thought about this for a moment and said with curiosity and amazement, "Did 'Abdu'l-Bahá do this for everyone?"

"Yes," said Palo, "He's our teacher and an example of how we should live our lives every day."

Dearest Cara replied with a peaceful smile, "I *really* want to be like 'Abdu'l-Bahá."

Palo laughed and said, "Me too, Dearest Cara! *Me too!*"

Chapter 8

Rags and the Virtue of Truthfulness

Rags is a very special dog that lives with Dearest Cara and her family in Wonderfuland. He has creamy vanilla fur and likes to wear a red bandana around his neck. His front and back legs are strong. Rags has big muscles from many years of travelling on the open road. More than once, Rags had to make a quick getaway from people who were not kind to him. His strong legs helped him to escape from some meanies on more than one occasion.

Dearest Cara and Poppy found Rags on a street corner in the town of Brattleboro. When they met him he was singing for his supper and did not have a home. Dearest Cara and Rags became quick friends and she brought him to live in Wonderfuland.

It goes without saying that Rags loves Dearest Cara with all his heart and soul. He has taken it upon himself to be Dearest Cara's personal bodyguard, even though she does not need one when she is in Wonderfuland. Rags always keep one ear pointed up to listen for trouble, even when he is asleep! He is always ready to protect and defend Dearest Cara and the other animal friends.

One sunny spring morning Dearest Cara, Rags, Penny, Sparky, Highway Kitty, and Sky were all playing in the meadow. Dearest Cara was pretending to be a deer and put some broken tree branches in her hair to look like a deer's antlers. She and the animal friends were dancing and chasing after each other. Everyone was having a fun time playing and pretending.

Sky was imagining she was performing in a circus and began doing her acrobatic wind-dance. She began doing loops and spins and was not paying attention to where she was going. She was so caught up in her performance that she accidentally flew over and outside the old picket fence bordering Wonderfuland!

When Dearest Cara saw Sky fly over the fence, she became very frightened. Sky Bird had flown out of Dearest Cara's sight and strayed into the thick and dark woods nearby.

Dearest Cara cried out, "Sky, come back!"

But little Sky was having so much fun doing her wind-dance and she did not hear Dearest Cara. Against her better judgment Dearest Cara climbed over the old picket fence and ran after Sky into the nearby woods.

Dearest Cara ran as fast as she could to catch up to Sky and shouted, "Sky, turn around! Hurry, you have flown outside of Wonderfuland. Come back!"

Realizing that things did not look familiar, Sky suddenly stopped in the air and turned around to see Dearest Cara running toward her calling out her name. Dearest Cara stopped and lifted her finger up into the air. Sky Bird gave out a little warble of relief and flew down and perched on Dearest Cara's outstretched finger.

In her high pitched warble, Sky said, "Dearest Cara, I don't know what happened! I was having so much fun doing my wind-dance. I must have flown over the fence by accident!"

Dearest Cara was out of breath from chasing Sky and panted, "I'm... just glad... you finally... heard me, Sky. We must... return to Wonderfuland... right away!"

Right about this time it just so happened that an old wolf—which was known to lurk around the borders of Wonderfuland—appeared a few yards away from behind an old dead tree. The wolf began to growl as he crept into the clearing where Dearest Cara and Sky had stopped to catch their breath. Dearest Cara and Sky froze as the old wolf locked its eyes on the two friends.

Dearest Cara was very frightened and whispered, "Sky, don't move." But poor little Sky could not control herself and began to tremble.

The wolf, having poor eye sight due to his old age, squinted to see just exactly who had stumbled across his path.

In a low growl he said, "What's this? A young deer alone in the woods? I know what I'm having for dinner tonight, hee hee hee."

Dearest Cara began to shake with fright! Remember, Dearest Cara was still dressed like a deer and had two branches poking out of her hair like antlers. The old wolf with his bad eyesight thought Dearest Cara was a real deer and started licking his chops as he crept closer to Dearest Cara and Sky.

Now, don't worry because Rags had been quick to follow Dearest Cara's scent as soon as she had disappeared from the animal friends playing in the meadow. With lightning speed, Rags ran up from behind Dearest Cara and Sky and leapt in between them and the old wolf.

Rags barked at the wolf, "Away with you, old wolfie! This young deer is a human girl and will be no lunch for you this day! Back into the woods with you! Go eat a pine cone for dinner!"

The old wolf was taken by complete surprise. He let out a whimper and scurried back into the woods with his tail tucked between his legs. Taking a deep breath, Dearest Cara and Rags ran back towards Wonderfuland with Sky leading the way.

Once over the old picket fence and back inside of Wonderfuland, Dearest Cara wrapped her arms around Rags and squeezed him with all her might.

"Thank you for rescuing us, Rags. Sky and I were so afraid. Your bravery saved us!"

Rags smiled and humbly said, "My Dearest Cara, I love you so very, very much. I'll always protect you!" He gave Dearest Cara a big slurp on her cheek.

By now, all the other animal friends had gathered around Dearest Cara and Rags. Sky perched on one of Dearest Cara's antler branches.

Dearest Cara's eyes opened wide and said, "I need to go and tell Momsy and Poppy about what just happened. I'm not allowed to go over the fence and outside of Wonderfuland without them. I'm scared to tell them that I did this because I disobeyed them. But I think I need to tell them the *truth* right now."

Dearest Cara started running and waved her hand for the animal friends to follow.

Dearest Cara led the way as the group ran up the hill to the little red cottage. She rushed into the living room and told Momsy and Poppy about her and Sky's encounter with the wolf. She told them how Sky accidently flew over the old picket fence and went outside of Wonderfuland into the dark woods and how she ran after Sky. She then told her parents about the old wolf who thought she was a deer and wanted to eat her for dinner!

Momsy and Poppy let out a big gasp when they heard this last part and Momsy clutched her hand over her heart, crying out, "Goodness gracious!" and almost fainted.

Poppy quickly grabbed Momsy before she hit the floor. In a very serious voice Poppy asked, "Dearest Cara, you know that you are not allowed to go outside of Wonderfuland without us. Why didn't you come get us when Sky Bird flew over the fence?"

Dearest Cara's big blue eyes looked down at the floor and said, "I'm sorry, I know I should have. I just wanted to bring Sky back into Wonderfuland. But not to worry Momsy and Poppy, Rags followed us over the fence and into the woods and chased off the mean old wolf."

Momsy and Poppy held Dearest Cara tightly in their arms. They told her how much they loved her and they were very pleased that she told them the *truth* about what happened. They gave Rags a large milk bone and a big hug for protecting Dearest Cara and Sky from the wolf. Rags smiled and wagged his tail, happy that his Dearest Cara was safe. Momsy and Poppy reminded Dearest Cara never to go over the old picket fence without them. Dearest Cara said she would never do it again and she meant it.

That night, before crawling into bed, Dearest Cara opened her window and leaned out to gaze at the stars and tell Palo about what happened earlier that day.

Dearest Cara said, "Palo, I think I've learned more about the virtue of *truthfulness* today. I learned that even when I may be scared to tell the *truth*, it's always important to be *truthful*.

"Yes! Yes!" said Palo, "Bahá'u'lláh tells us:

...*Let truthfulness and courtesy be your adorning.*

Dearest Cara looked at Palo and asked, "What does *adorning* mean?

"*Adorning* is another word for *wearing* something, like a hat or a coat or scarf. Think of it like this..." said Palo, "when Momsy puts flowers in your hair, she's adding something beautiful to your appearance. She's *adorning* you with flowers. So when we're *truthful*, we're *adorning* ourselves with a beautiful virtue. We're adding something beautiful to ourselves—both on the outside and on the inside."

Dearest Cara said, "So when we practice the virtue of *truthfulness*, we become more beautiful inside, too? Even when we can't see it?

"Yes!" Palo replied. "Even when you don't see it, others will see it, and most importantly God will see it."

Thinking about *truthfulness*, Dearest Cara looked into the night sky with its millions of stars sparkling brightly and closed her eyes. Dearest Cara quietly gave her heart to Bahá'u'lláh and thanked Him for all the many blessings in her life.

As she opened her eyes she felt a wave of peace flow over her. The scared feelings she had felt earlier began to disappear. She climbed under her covers and Rags hopped up on the bed and snuggled next to her. Penny, Sparky, and Highway Kitty joined them on the bed. Sky perched herself on the headboard above Dearest Cara and Rags. Dearest Cara wrapped her arms around Rags and whispered into his ear, "I love you so much, Rags."

Within a few minutes they both fell into a deep sleep and Dearest Cara dreamt about a glorious paint set that had all the colors of a rainbow. Rags dreamt about tasty milk-bone dog biscuits dancing in the air.

Chapter 9

Will and the Virtue of Detachment

One day, Dearest Cara was meditating on Whale Rock, wondering about how to be happy without wanting anything. She began thinking about what Palo had told her the previous night before bedtime: *worldly things come and go, but spiritual qualities are forever!*

Sitting cross-legged in the warm morning sun, Dearest Cara began thinking about being happy. She said to herself out loud, "I would be so very happy if I could get that paint set from the art store in town. The paint set comes with so many pretty colors.....turquoise, magenta, orange, green, and light blue!"

Dearest Cara's eyes got very big and bright as she thought about all the beautiful colors in the paint set. She shouted with much excitement, "Oh, how I love to paint! I'd be so happy if Momsy would buy that paint set for me."

As Dearest Cara thought more and more about the paint set, she became frustrated and sad. She said out loud, "I can't seem to save my allowance. I always end up spending all of it on sweet treats from Wilgoshes,"

Her voice became louder as she started to name her favorite sweet treats from Wilgoshes, "...apple cakes with brown sugar frosting...fruit smoothies with loads of berries, yogurt sundaes with fruit and nut toppings...oh how I love those sweet treats from Wilgoshes!"

Suddenly Dearest Cara came back to reality.

"Momsy and Poppy say I have to learn to save my allowance if I want a new paint set. How I spend my allowance is my choice and I must accept the choices I make."

As she closed her eyes and thought about the paint set, she heard a beautiful melody coming from up above. She opened her eyes, stood up, and looked upward and saw a bright red cardinal staring down at her.

Dearest Cara said to the bird, "Hello, Mr. Bird. You sure do have the most wonderful bird-song! What's your name, sir?"

The red cardinal looked down at Dearest Cara and replied, "My name is Wilhelm, but my friends call me Will."

"Can I become your friend and call you Will, too?" asked Dearest Cara with a hopeful smile.

"Yes, Of course! What's your name young lady?" said Will.

Dearest Cara answered, "My name is Dearest Cara, and my friends call me Dearest Cara."

Will chuckled and replied, "That's easy to remember!

He continued, "I could not help but over hear what you said about the difficult choice you have to make between the sweet treats and the paint set."

Dearest Cara nodded and said in a sad voice, "Yes, Will. I've had a hard time saving my allowance for a paint set. I end up spending it all on sweet treats at Wilgoshes every week."

Will agreed, "Hmmmmm that's quite a predicament."

"*Preee-dic-a-ment*...what does that word mean?" asked Dearest Cara in a puzzled tone.

"Oh, predicament is just a fancy word for *problem*."

He continued, "I find when we try to see the end in the beginning, it sometimes can help us to make wise choices. For example, instead of just focusing on the moment, such as when you want a sweet treat, try to imagine yourself with the paint set, see the colors and paint brush in your hand...imagine the feelings of happiness you have when you paint. This is seeing the end in the beginning. It will help you to control spending all your allowance on sweet treats at this Wilgoshes place you keep mentioning."

"Oh Wilgoshes is a little store down the road from Wonderfuland. They have the best sweet treats in the whole, wide world!" replied Cara smacking her lips with a big grin. She then thought a moment about the words Will had shared with her.

Dearest Cara had an idea! She jumped up with much excitement and exclaimed, "Thank you, Will! You are very wise. I will try to see the end in the beginning!"

Will added, "Yes! When you do this, it can help you develop *detachment*."

Dearest Cara repeated the word, "*Detachment*, I'll remember this new word!"

She then jumped off Whale Rock onto the bank of the Rock River. She waved goodbye to

Will and thanked him again for his wise words. She was so happy she did a little cartwheel and ran to play with her animal friends who had gathered nearby in the meadow.

That night Dearest Cara was very excited to tell Palo about her new friend, Will the Cardinal. She explained to Palo how Will had suggested she save her allowance to buy the paint set.

Dearest Cara asked Palo, "Will told me about *detachment*. Is *detachment* like not wanting anything?

"Well kind of... *detachment* is a virtue that all of us need to learn and strengthen. It is very helpful to learn *detachment* when we are young. *Detachment* is learning how to wait patiently for things we want, or even learning to accept that we do not always get everything we want. By strengthening the virtue of *detachment*, we strengthen control over our self, and thereby strengthen our spirituality."

"I don't understand Palo," replied Dearest Cara in a confused voice.

"Well, let me see if I can help you understand." said Palo.

"Sometimes, when we are able to let go of wanting something so strongly we can replace that wanting with relying on what God wants for us. We must try and remember that what God wants for us is always what is best for us. When we practice the virtue of *detachment*, we are making room in our hearts for what God wants for us, rather than what we want. This helps us to grow closer to God and strengthens us spiritually. `Abdu'l-Bahá says in one of my favorite prayers, *Oh God My God! Fill up for me the cup of detachment from all things...*"

Dearest Cara said in wonderment, "So, to practice *detachment*, I'll try and save my allowance for the paint set and not spend it on the sweet treats at Wilgoshes. I'll have to wait longer to get the paint set, but this will make the virtue of *detachment* grow stronger in me. When I'm more *detached*, I'll have stronger self-control. This will help me to grow spiritually closer to God. Does that sound right, Palo?"

"That sounds very right to me Dearest Cara! I think you've got it! " said Palo with a big smile.

That night as Dearest Cara drifted off to sleep, she imagined all the pretty pictures she would paint in Wonderfuland when she bought her new paint set. She thought more about *detachment* and felt a warm feeling in her heart as she thought about this virtue helping her to grow closer to God.

Chapter 10

Good Night in Wonderfuland

As the sun sets and the blanket of night slowly falls over Wonderfuland, Dearest Cara, Momsy, Poppy and all the animal friends gather together to say their evening prayers before bedtime. After prayers Dearest Cara and her animal friends all settle down in their favorite sleeping spots and are kissed good-night by Momsy and Poppy.

You can find Penny, under the covers, snuggled up closely on Dearest Cara's right side. On her left side, Sparky sprawls across the pillow leaning up against Dearest Cara's head. Highway Kitty is tucked close to Sparky. Sky Bird is perched on Dearest Cara's head while Will the Cardinal, finds his spot on the bed post nearby. Rags sprawls comfortably on his back on the floor, knowing all is safe and secure with one ear up, always watchful over Dearest Cara, even in his sleep.

As everyone in the little red cottage begins to drift off to sleep, Whale Rock glistens silently under the star-lit sky. Water flows over stones in the Rock River creating a beautiful melody and this song gently lulls all in Wonderfuland to sleep. Sweet fragrances from the meadow mix with the perfume of Tajalli Rose bush as the cool night breeze blows in through the cottage windows. All is well in Wonderfuland.... All is peaceful in Wonderfuland... All are loved in Wonderfuland... *Good Night*!